Poskitt's Puzzles

THE MYSTERY OF THE MAGIC TOY

by Kjartan Poskitt

illustrated by David Higham

IDEALS CHILDREN'S BOOKS
Nashville, Tennessee

Mr. Belcher has been clearing out his attic.

He has found a huge collection of his old toys.
One of them is very special because it's

MAGIC

The trouble is, he can't remember which one it is,
so will you help him?

The Mystery of the Magic Toy lies in this book.

First published in U.S. 1989 by Ideals Publishing Corp., Nashville, Tennessee
in association with Belitha Press Limited,
31 Newington Green, London N16 9PU
Text and illustrations in this format © Belitha Press 1989
Text copyright © Kjartan Poskitt 1989
Illustrations copyright © David Higham 1989
ISBN 0-8249-8380-7 (softcover)
ISBN 0-8249-8406-4 (hardcover)
Printed in Hong Kong for Imago Publishing

First of all, you must turn the page
and see all the toys sitting in his attic.

Look at them all very carefully and try
to remember as much as you can!
When you have done that, turn to the
next page and find out what to do next.

4

5

On every page in this book is a clue to the Magic Toy.

The clue will also ask you a question, then tell you to turn to another page for the next clue.

If you can remember everything as you go along, you will find out which is the Magic Toy!

Ready? Then here's your first question.

What was in between the tennis racket and the blocks?

If you think it was the teddy bear, turn to page **21**.

If you don't, then turn to page **16**.

Mr. Belcher tried the flags but found they couldn't flap about with no wind! One of them has gotten lost, though.

If you think it's turn to page **22**.

But if you think it's turn to page **18**.

These are Mr. Belcher's blocks.
Sadly, they don't make magic castles.
He has one of each shape.

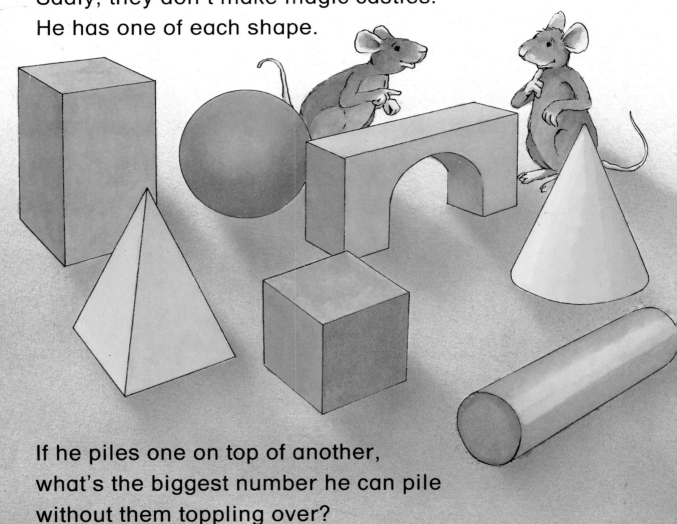

If he piles one on top of another,
what's the biggest number he can pile
without them toppling over?

If you think it's five, turn to page **17**.
If you think it's six, turn to page **21**.

The airplane cannot fly by itself, and the books do not contain magic spells. Which was higher up in the attic?

If it was the plane, then turn to page **18**.
If it was the books, turn to page **11**.

Mr. Belcher now thinks he knows which toy is

MAGIC

Do you know too?
If so, turn to page **24** and check.

But... warning!

The Magic Toy is clever.
It has changed the picture
on page **24** to disguise itself!
DON'T BELIEVE WHAT YOU SEE!

The doll cannot cry real tears.

What was placed among the soldiers?

If you think it was the ball,
turn to page **21**.

If you think it was the teddy bear,
turn to page **18**.

Now turn to page **21**.

Now turn to page **7**.

Now turn to page **11**.

The bucket and shovel
cannot make magic sandcastles.

How many cars was the train pulling?

If you think it was seven, turn to page **9**.

Otherwise turn to page **8**.

The teddy bear cannot
do a magic dance.

Which paw was dangling off the attic shelf?

Was it the right paw?
Turn to page **19**.

Or was it the left paw?
Turn to page **11**.

The chess set cannot play a magic
game by itself.

What was on the floor behind it?

If you think it was the bucket and shovel,
turn to page **11**.

If not, turn to page **14**.

The tennis racket cannot hit the ball by magic.

What was on the shelf between the truck and the teddy bear?

If you think it was the dartboard, turn to page **18**.

If not, turn to page **20**.

The doll cannot talk with a magic voice.

What was on the attic floor directly below the flags?

If you think it was the tennis racket, turn to page **9**.

If you think it was the bucket and shovel, turn to page **21**.

Neither the dartboard nor the racing car are magic.

Mr. Belcher has found three more soldiers, but only one matches the others on the shelf.

Choose the one you think it is, then turn to the page indicated.

page
10

page
21

page
16

The airplane cannot fly by magic power.

Which was nearer the train set,
the racing car or the truck?

Turn to page **23** for the racing car
or page **9** if you think it was the truck.

Neither the soldiers nor the train set are magic.

How many darts were there in the dartboard?

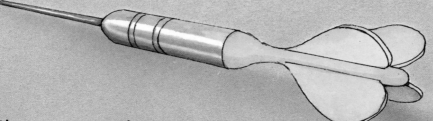

If you think there were three, turn to page **9**.

If you think there were four, turn to page **11**.

The ball cannot magically roll home.

Mr. Belcher has straightened his books.
They are numbered and in a row . . .
but in the wrong order!

How many books does he need to move
to get them all in the correct order?

If you think it's three, turn to page **15**.

If you think it's four, turn to page **18**.

22

Mr. Belcher has lost some of his toys in a maze.

He walks through the maze, *turning right* at every junction he comes to. Every toy he walks past is not magic.

To help Mr. Belcher through the magic maze, turn to pages **12** and **13**.

If you have answered all the questions correctly, you should know which toys are *not* magic. So you should know the one remaining toy *is* magic.

Stumped? Try working the puzzle again. Be sure to read only the clues on the pages that you turn to, and pay careful attention to the maze and illustrations.

If you've got it right, *well done!*

You could now tell Mr. Belcher that you've found his Magic Toy!

Give up? Send a self-addressed, stamped envelope to: Poskitt's Answers, Ideals Publishing Corporation, Nelson Place at Elm Hill Pike, P.O. Box 140300, Nashville, Tennessee 37214